SILENT MAGIC

United Twinkle Sisters Adventure

K.J. KING

To Kyle & Jacquelyn—my kids—my heart<3

CONTENTS

United Twinkle Sisters
Awaken within magical twisters
We are powerful, free
Charmed are we
My sisters and me

One of mist so clear and fine
Two joins in and bends the time
Three who shifts and changes shape
Fourth holds a secret she can't escape

Our powers together, we will swirl
When connected begin to twirl
Expanding, growing tenfold
the time is now, behold

United Twinkle Sisters power
Protecting Earth we shall shower
We cover life that is dear
Preventing the end so near

Our love and light we brightly shine
To create a new age on Earth divine
Twinkle Twinkle my sisters and me
United, powerful, charmed are we

CHAPTER 1

Misty, the eldest sister, has been here since time began. But now she is missing. At least Echo feels like she is. Misty isn't answering Echo's calls, which has never happened before. Echo is the youngest of the four cosmic sisters in this lifetime. Age is calculated in linear time here on Earth, but in the cosmic world, the sisters are old souls. They have had many human experiences in preparation for the mission they have been given in this lifetime. Confusing? We know.

"Misty has gone off my radar," Echo says to herself with a deep sigh as she sits outside on her back porch. One of her favorite spots to relax. Echo was born with this internal knowing

—a deep inner connection to all the people she loves. It is not a knowing as in where they are, or what they are doing per se, just a knowing if they are safe or not. She calls it her radar because she feels their essence like a blip on a radar screen. It has been a week or more since she visited with Misty. Misty is no longer in her human form in this lifetime. Actually, none of the sisters remember her in a human form, not even in previous lifetimes.

As Echo sits quietly remembering the past few months and trying to figure out where Misty may have disappeared to, she realizes the time. "Oh my, I really need to get packed. I am going to meet my sisters tomorrow," Echo says out loud, then she chuckles at herself and shakes her head, as she is alone.

These past few months continue to unfold quietly in her mind, like the sun setting on an amazing day. She releases another deep sigh. Smiling to herself, she thinks, *I'm blessed. My life is so wonderful, magical even, but now bittersweet. I finally get to meet all my sisters in person tomorrow, and I am so excited.*

Here on Earth, the days must come to an end, and as the sun sinks down into the darkness of the sky, displaying many colors along the way, Echo finds herself still sitting on the back porch of her ranch. She feels so much joy to meet her sisters, but at the same time, a bit melancholy as this could be the last time she will enjoy the beautiful Texas sunsets. She is prepared for their mission and whatever is to come. Life as they all know it is about to change drastically.

You see, their sisterhood began before Earth was created. It all started with the proverbial Cosmic Big Bang, or simply put, a creative idea. Everything comes from Source Energy which has no beginning or end, and to our best understanding, just expanded into the universe, creating Earth, creating us, all that is or will ever be. It sounds futuristic, but it is real.

Source Energy is the creator of all universal laws, which are science, math, physics, and more. All souls that come to Earth come to learn, grow, and expand. The cosmic sisters were sent here many times knowing they had a purpose. However, they were not aware of just how important their purpose would be, and they didn't know about their sisterhood until the time was exactly right for them to reunite. That time is Now.

Raven, Syd, and Echo have lived here on Earth—they have had many lifetimes learning lessons—some long forgotten, others they remember. Misty, well, she is everywhere and nowhere all at the same time. She appears whenever she is needed. The cosmic sisters required many lifetimes to master their unique gifts which will allow them to finally complete their mission. This mission was revealed to each of them when they met Misty at the beginning of the year. Echo remembers it was late, on a very dark night. She was sitting outside gazing at the stars as she often does, when a strange mist floated in from the north, it was mesmerizing. Echo had never noticed mist rolling in the skies of west Texas. It was as if the mist knew what Echo was feeling, it changed direction and moved straight to her, enveloping Echo, like a giant hug—surprisingly warm. She heard a quiet, silky rich voice, "Echo, it's Misty. Do you remember me?" In an instant, a memory of long, long ago awakens inside Echo's brain, she feels as if she is whisked back in time.

"I was an Elf-Faerie living in Ireland in 1846, I was in human form, and I had lost my entire family to starvation and was taken in as a servant to a royal family. It was here in their castle I was able to practice a few of my gifts, shifting time forward or back, having conversations with all things not human, and mastering the ability to blend in with nature, becoming almost invisible. This is where I began to discover that even though I had many gifts, shifting time or blending in were the most important of all. As a mere peasant in the castle, my duties were to clean the living quarters which allowed me to move freely about the castle, unnoticed and alone. The nobles never acknowledged peasants; we were there to serve. I knew that I could take many forms when desired, which is one truthful legend about faeries that has carried through the ages.

"This life as a peasant allowed me many opportunities to practice my magical gifts. I could become invisible to humans if I so desired. I discovered this ability out of sheer necessity, if I was seen performing my duties, I would be punished severely or worse; banished forever, left to starve, wither away and die. It was always so cold in that castle. The cold would sink deep into my bones." Echo wonders if she has carried that memory with her through the ages, as she now prefers hot weather, like Texas summers or the Caribbean beach life. The memory continues to unfold in her mind as if it is happening now.

"One morning, as I was cleaning up the princess's bedroom chambers, she happened to return to her room. Most often, if this happened, I could quickly become invisible by blending in, as we faeries often do, leaving without being noticed. On this particular day, Princess was quite angry and slammed her bedroom door, which left me trapped, I didn't dare risk opening the doorway and creating a 'ghost in the castle' which—I digress—is another story for another time.

"I stayed small and invisible in the corner of the room as I did not want her to bump into me either. As I watched Princess pace around her room, ranting and raving, which soon turned to tears, she sat down and began to sob. My heart was so full of love for her and I wanted to grant her wish, heal her pain. However, I took a vow not to interfere with free will. All I could do was remain hidden behind the shield I created which was depleting my energy.

"I was wrecked, exhausted. I knew that

given the state Princess was in, if she discovered me, I would be forever banished from the castle. In this moment, I was not aware of how much time had passed, but I knew it had to be a long time because I had just begun my chores for the day and now the sun was beginning to set. Shannon, her chambermaid, entered the room to lay out Princess's bed clothes and light candles for her. If I didn't know better, I would swear Shannon saw me. She was ever so careful in placing the candles to avoid lighting up the corner where I hid. It was in that instant I saw time reverse, and I was standing alone, chatting with the most delightful yellow flowers that had been placed upon her dressing table. That was when I realized I had bent time more than I ever had before. With no time to think, I quickly scampered out of the chambers to safety as I heard Princess coming up the stairs ranting to herself.

"I finished my chores for the day and escaped to my secret hiding spot in the castle. I needed to practice this amazing gift: bending time. As I grew weary, ready to rest my body, I stepped outside into the courtyard, the quickest route to the servants' chambers. Thinking I could risk it this late at night. As I stepped outside, the door closed behind me before I realized the courtyard was lit up in all its glory by the full moon smiling down. With all that had taken place that day, I had forgotten about the moon phases.

"I tried—unsuccessfully—to open the locked door. I attempted to raise my shield, blend into the wall; however, I did not have the energy reserves to blend. I looked out across the courtyard, desperately trying to figure out how I was going to cross, and noticed some members of the royal family standing on the path. I leaned up against the door, staying in the shadows, becoming as small as I possibly could in hopes they would continue their journey in the opposite direction. But instead they were headed straight for the door.

"I closed my eyes, taking in deep breaths, searching and searching for an answer, a way out. I could not be discovered, and I did not want to explain how I happened to be out in the courtyard, which was absolutely forbidden to all servants. As I stood shivering in the shadows, unable to discover any way out of this moment, a mist rolled in like a giant red carpet covering the courtyard and growing in size and thickness to such a thick fog, I could barely see my own hands.

"I then felt a warmth cover me; I caught a glimpse of the most fascinating sparkle of brown eyes I had ever seen, and I heard barely a whisper in my ear: "Follow me, dear Echo." Deep in my soul, the knowing was there. The knowing that I should follow even though, at the time, I did not know where this mist came from, I always knew and felt safe, warm, guided. Of course, my sister, Misty, once again led me away from danger to safety. Misty, always clear on what path I needed to follow, always full of unconditional love, never judging my mistakes, never telling me what I should do, only guiding me to safety. All I need to do is take that step and follow. Echo has lived a long life in Ireland, strengthening her gifts of bending time and space. She has so many fond memories of interesting beings she met along the way.

"YES! Oh, Misty, of course, I remember you," Echo says as she begins to see Misty's face take shape within the mist. She wears a turban of white which is so bright against her beautiful brown skin, her brown eyes sparkle and glimmer with specks of gold that twinkle like the stars of the night. Misty begins to reveal information about a New Age—a paradigm shift—that has started. She explains to Echo that she will be part of a mission later this year. "You still have much to learn. The first step will be to sign up for a Spiritual online course. Echo, you must complete the course, it will help you release your human-ness, and any blocks that might prevent you from connecting deeper to your authentic self. I will reveal more information later, if you agree to do as I say."

"Yes, Misty, I trust you completely," Echo answers.

"Echo, it is imperative you start first thing tomorrow morning, it will help you grow to new levels. Once completed, I will reveal the next steps, do you understand?" Misty's voice is only a whisper as her face fades into the mist. The warmth and love is indescribable as it continues to envelop Echo, she feels her own tears stream down her face. It was in this meeting that Echo realized Misty was not only her guide since, well, forever, but she is her oldest sister.

Echo registered for the course the next day, and it was there in the online classroom that she met Raven and Obsidian. They had an instant connection, the kind when you meet someone and feel as if you have known them forever. They were able to study together, but most importantly, get to know each other.

Obsidian was lovingly nicknamed Syd by Echo and Raven, as it suits her better. In their chats online, they began sharing knowledge of their past lives and the special gifts they each were given. These gifts they were never able to openly share with family and friends. They knew they would think they were crazy because most humans believe that magic isn't real—it is only pretend. Oh, if they only knew! They hope that soon the world will know there is a bit of magic in everyone. They discovered they had all been guided by Misty to take this course, and realized in that moment, they were sisters; Cosmic sisters.

It feels unbelievable at times, very hard to wrap my Earthly human mind around this, and yet my soul, the true essence of me, knows it to be truth, more true than anything I have ever known. I feel it in my bones, Echo thinks to herself, which makes her laugh out loud again. Knowing they are not alone; they are all connected to each other—this amazing group of women filled with such indescribable love for each other.

As the weeks went by, and they were nearing completion of the online course, Misty visited each one of them, revealing the first leg of this journey of many to come on their cosmic sister-hood mission.

Echo realizes she is shivering; the temperature has dropped. It must be late. She was lost in remembering some of the stories from her past. Standing, she stretches her tall, lean body—her mind still racing with all that has happened this past year. She takes deep breaths to quiet her mind, she is not afraid of the mission, as it has to be done, there is no way around it. She knows it is human nature feeling the need to sift through all the information to be prepared. She shakes her head and takes a few more deep breaths to clear her mind. She knows over-thinking solves nothing. *Trust yourself and jump!* Echo thinks, for she does trust herself, Misty, and her sisters completely.

Echo gazes up at the stars, stretching one last time, and goes inside to finish packing. She hears a soft knock at the side door; it has to be Jake, her ranch hand, because her heart always races faster whenever he is near. "Come in, Jake," Echo yells out as she heads toward the door.

Jake almost has to duck coming in, as he is 6' 7, a solid mass of muscles, all manly-ness, and moviestar handsome. "Just checking in with you, I will be ready at five to take you to the airport. All is well, I just made my rounds, and put the horses in for the night. We are expecting a cold front," Jake tells Echo in his delightful, deep, southern voice. Jake always has a smile on his face and an accent all his own; part Texan and part, well, just full-on Jake charisma.

Echo still has a hard time slowing her heart beat. Without realizing it, she lays her hand over her heart, feeling giddy as a school girl, she tells him, "Thank you, Jake, see ya in the morning for coffee!"

"Goodnight, Echo," Jake says, pulling the door closed behind him. Echo leans against the wall, feeling weak in the knees. She could swear he just winked at her . . . nah, just wishful thinking.

While packing her clothes, her mind wanders back to the day she met Jake. She remembers: She was at the airport on her way to San Francisco to meet her best friend, Liza, for a much-needed girls trip. It was very early in the morning, she was dressed in her comfy clothes, way too casual, planning to change and freshen up once she arrived.

Liza wasn't scheduled to land until a few hours after. She literally woke up and left, no makeup, hair stuffed under her ratty baseball cap. Of course, her makeup bag was in her luggage which was hopefully loaded onto the airplane. Sitting at the gate, reading her book, certainly not looking her best, she heard a rich, deep, southern accent. It immediately sent her heart racing.

Echo looked up to see who this voice belonged to, but had to keep looking up because this man was big and tall and . . . whoa . . . all cowboy! He walked back and forth in his Stetson hat, white shirt, jeans, and cowboy boots while talking on the phone to someone he called Baby. *Dang, of course, he is married.*

Echo remembers how silly she felt, she certainly was not about to start a relationship, anyway. That would be a great way to grab attention: "Hi, I'm Echo, spiritual guru on a mission to save the world from ending." Talk about bringing some baggage into a relationship!

Shortly after their encounter, the intercom announced the plane was boarding, and in Echo fashion, she had forgotten to reserve a seat, so she was one of the last to board. As her section was called, she put her book into her backpack and joined the line, looking around hoping for one last glimpse of that tall drink of handsome cowboy, but he was nowhere in sight.

Echo boarded the plane. Inching her way along the aisle, she heard, "I saved you a seat." *WHAT!? Could it be?* Echo looked over to her right and saw the cowboy pointing to the seat next to him. *I may have just won the lottery.*

"Hi, I'm Jake Callahan!" He smiled—of course, a perfect smile—beautiful, golden, tanned skin and the dreamiest brown eyes with little flecks of gold in them. Puppy dog eyes.

"Hi Jake, I'm Echo," she said awkwardly, attempting to remove her backpack. Jake immediately helped her with it. Echo wanted to pinch herself; this had to be a dream. They had that instant soulmate connection all romance novels are made of. As the plane began take off, Echo had a moment of tension; she tended toward motion sickness and hates flying. Jake reached over to cover her hand with his. Echo looked down to see because her hand felt like a tiny child's compared to his. Her heart skipped a few beats, she felt such love in his touch.

To her surprise, she discovered he was not married, he was speaking with his niece, he had plans to move back to Texas and was on his way to California to finalize the sale of his home and business in LA. Such a wonderful memory. The beginning of their beautiful friendship and now working relationship.

Echo hired Jake to run her ranch while she was gone. Of course, she has not shared the real reason for her travels, she just told him she would be traveling with her sisters on a very long, much needed vacation. Echo finishes packing and jumps into bed. She has to be up very early tomorrow morning. As she falls asleep, she is smiling, dreaming of Jake.

CHAPTER 2

The ride to the airport is uneventful, discussing ranch business is the only way Echo can remain focused this morning. Jake pulls up to the outdoor check in; always the perfect gentleman, he jumps out to open Echo's door, then unloads her luggage and hands it to the porter at check in. He swallows Echo up into his gigantic arms, which is unexpected as Echo always keeps things all business. "I will miss you, Echo, please check in with me occasionally so I know y'all are safe," Jake says quietly as he continues to hug her. Echo can't help but melt into him. She is tiny compared to him, and she struggles to remain standing.

"Okay, bye," is all she manages to say as she

turns to the luggage porter and hands him her passport. Echo cannot bear to look up at Jake; she doesn't want him to see the tears forming in her eyes. She grabs her boarding pass and heads into the airport never looking back even though she can feel Jake staring at her.

❧

ECHO DOESN'T REALIZE JAKE SOMEHOW knows this might be the last time he sees her, a part of him wants to run after her. He wants to make her tell him what is going on. It takes all of his willpower to stop himself as he jumps back into his truck and takes off faster than he should, mumbling under his breath, "Dear God, let her be safe. She has no idea she is my everything."

As Jake takes the long drive back to the ranch, he remembers the many discussions he has shared with Echo over the past few months. His smile returns as he drives through the amazing Hill country of Texas, remembering how the last several months have been the very best in his life. So many times he wanted to share with Echo how he feels about her but as soon as he would begin to talk about it, she would immediately change the topic. He could feel her pull away, never sure of why, so he continues to give her the space she needs, hoping she will open up to him one day.

ECHO BOARDS THE PLANE FIRST, THANKS TO Jake. He not only takes care of the ranch, he takes care of Echo. She finally lets the tears fall, allowing all the feelings she has for Jake to flow through her. She knows this is the only way she can let go of them as she says her last silent goodbye to him. She feels overwhelmed by her mission and allows herself a moment of 'why me.' *Why little 'ol me, Echo, a small town Texas girl, could be given a mission as large as this is mind boggling. To save the world, really? Me?* How could this be happening now, when she has finally met the man she has dreamed about, like forever . . . why now?

Thirteen crystal skulls were hidden long ago on Earth, the mission is to locate them and bring them to a hidden safe place. Honestly, that is the mission, but for their safety—as well as the skulls'—it was agreed that Misty would reveal only enough information for each journey.

This first skull is hidden in the Mayan ruins in Cancun. Echo, Syd, and Raven will begin their adventure today. Echo feels ready in many ways, Misty has given them the knowledge they need to locate the first skull. Echo gathers her strength, quieting her mind now as the plane takes off. She thinks about Misty again, wondering if she is possibly preparing and that is why Echo could not reach her.

Even though Echo doesn't fully understand where Misty comes from or goes to without a body, maybe—just maybe—it takes her awhile to prepare to show up in Cancun. Echo's mind continues to race through many thoughts trying to figure out what she is about to do. Her human mind, or the ego, which is a portion of the brain that helps keep us safe when needed, oftentimes creates false fears keeping one stuck in the human condition.

Echo was able to stop the useless mind chatter a long time ago, but she can not fault the ego now, because if they fail, the world will end. Misty would not reveal if it will end as in a big bang—poof, everything is gone including the planet—kind of way or end in a slow, falling apart, kind of way. The kind of ending that leaves you remembering how good things were. The kind of end like when your favorite cup cracks and no matter how many times you fix it, it will not hold the liquid anymore; it just seeps out of the cracks. Knowing it is useless to keep but sad to let go. Tossing it into the trash feels so final. The cup no longer works aside from holding the memories of a better time when you were free to sit and enjoy that steamy, hot cup of cocoa.

Echo feels relieved Misty doesn't tell them; it comforts her in an odd way. Besides, there are so many paths to getting there you can't really ever see the future; it is infinite—too many variables, too many paths, so many choices. Free will, that universal law that allows all of us to choose our own paths.

The sisters have been training for this since the Earth was created—each one very powerful with many gifts given them from intelli-source, God, the universe, whatever you choose to call Source energy. Add in the power of four together united, well, that is the strongest bond in all the galaxies that Source has ever created.

It is amazing; here we are in 2018, with all this technology, the world seems to have advanced in so many ways, and some humans here are still so, so primitive, unaware, sleep-walking through life. Very few are even aware of the magical energy all around them, most do not even know there are laws governing this universe they live in; or that there are so many other parallel worlds, other galaxies with planets of their own. They think it is science fiction— maybe they are better off, who knows?

Echo and her sisters know they are the chosen Cosmic Sisters on their first journey to locate the real crystal skulls, and she needs to quit thinking, to stay completely focused and connected to Source.

She knows they are powerful, she feels the power rolling through her entire being as if the human-ness can barely hold onto it all. She realizes others are beginning to notice. She used to move about this earth, blending in with the rest of the world, unnoticed the majority of the time. Now people stare at her, some move away like she has three heads. Others are drawn to her, thinking they know her from somewhere. What they may not realize is the fullness of source energy—pure love—that fills her every cell is what draws them to her like a magnet.

Every human being has a source connection; some call it your soul, others say spirit and some even think it is something you have outside of you. Not true. Every human being is created from Source. They do not know it, believing life happens to them, they are disconnected and lost in their mind chatter. Believing, day to day, that their life is a string of random events.

Others are connected, enlightened human beings, recognizing the energy, knowing it is from Source energy. Many are beginning to awaken and discover their gifts, but they are new souls not quite ready for the New Age. The few—like the sisters—are completely connected, expanding, fine-tuning their gifts, giving back to Mother Earth, taking care of her, loving, respecting all life forms on this planet. Everything is made from energy, and all energy is Source. We are connected to all energy. We are one. So it is.

The cosmic sisters have only known each other through their internet meetings. This sisterhood they share is an unbreakable vow they agreed upon when time began. They know each other so well now, as if they had grown up together. Echo already feels their blips on her radar and knows they are on their way to Cancun.

Oh, what an adventure we will have, she thinks to herself as she closes her eyes and meditates.

She begins by setting her intentions. *We will save the skulls and live in a beautiful new world, a world where there is no hate, only love.* She visualizes this place where they are all free to use their gifts here on Earth, raising the vibrations of the planet, healing Mother Earth.

In her mind's eye, Echo can see the vivid colors and all the magical creatures coming out of hiding. She begins to think about their mission and her sisters as every single atom in her body begins to vibrate pure love. Tears form again. This time they are happy tears as she feels the love and imagines such a beautiful world full of peace. She wishes she could show this vision to every human being so they, too, would know.

Alas, she cannot, as she knows she is not allowed to interfere with anyone's free will to choose their own path. Echo has her head-phones in, her eyes closed as she does not want to speak with anyone on the flight, partly because she is struggling to keep her mind quiet. She feels like she is a hot mess inside. She can not complete an intelligent thought right now, let alone carry on a conversation.

Wanting to blend in with the crowd, Echo is dressed in comfortable, casual clothes, traveling unnoticed. What she doesn't realize is, even without makeup, she is stunning. She is tall and lean from her daily practice of yoga and working on her ranch all these years, the sun has not damaged her olive skin as she still looks like a college student. She radiates so much love from within she literally glows. With her long, blonde hair, beautiful almond-shaped, blue eyes, and pouty lips, she looks like an angel.

Echo has trained for this journey since the beginning of time. So many memories continue to flood her mind even though she attempts to meditate. She knows she has to stop all thoughts, relaxing into her breathing and meditation. It is imperative she remains alert, on guard, always with a clear mind. She made sure she did not see or feel any empty faces following her as they drove out to the airport. *Failure is not an option,* is her last thought as she falls into her deep, meditative state.

Not long after dozing off, Echo is jolted out of meditation by Sami, the flight attendant. "Miss, we are about to land," Sami says to her kindly. Sami had handed Echo a box of Kleenex right after she had boarded the plane because she had noticed the tears on Echo's face.

Echo tells her thank you and smiles to let her know she is okay now. She then turns to look out the window as they circle above the beautiful Caribbean sea. *Oh, how the clear, tranquil, turquoise water speaks to my soul,* Echo thinks as she allows her connection to the sea to flow through her, bringing a deep peace and calmness within.

The plane lands, roughly taxiing into Cancun. Echo is the first to arrive, as her flight is just a little over two hours from San Antonio. Once Echo finds her luggage, she walks over to the rental car kiosk to pick up the SUV she reserved, thinking they will need the extra space to carry the equipment, supplies, and three ladies' luggage.

She leaves the airport in search of a grocery store and some type of sporting goods or hardware store. She will have everything ready when her sisters arrive. Thankfully, they were able to schedule their flights fairly close to one another's.

Echo is excited she discovers an app that allows her to watch their flights come in. She loves technology, it fascinates her. Growing up on a ranch she never had computers or cell phones, but once she went away to college she caught up with the world. She smiles to herself that she could get the app to work. She watches their flights land in real time.

CHAPTER 3

As she pulls the SUV into the curbside pickup line, she can hardly contain her excitement. Syd has flown in from England. In this life, Syd has the most delightful British accent. She is graceful, elegant, full of kindness with the most gentle spirit Echo has ever encountered. Her eyes are the color of the sky and seem to change from blue to gray to green depending on what she is chatting about.

Syd is the skull expert and has visited many skulls only to discover that they are quite exquisite replicas. Syd has felt drawn to the skulls since a young age and what began as an interest for her turned into research. She even wrote some fictional adventure books about them. Syd discovered the original skulls hidden long ago are, in fact, real, not just ghost tales or myth.

Misty has shared that Syd is the only one who can harness the energy force and reveal the knowledge within them, but we are still unclear on all the details. Misty explained to them that Syd had memory charms placed upon her to keep her and the skulls safe. When the time comes, she will remove them which will allow them to complete the mission. Syd thinks Misty becomes frustrated with her because sometimes she asks her a million questions. Misty always responds with that silky smooth voice, "All in good time," then she disappears off into the unknown realms.

Raven is flying in from Peru, she is originally from New York but doesn't technically live anywhere. She lives wherever she decides. If it were the 1970s, she would be described as a "hippie" or "gypsy." Raven is the most amazing free spirit, she has long, purple hair which highlights her beautiful topaz-colored eyes, girlish freckles across her nose, and her brilliant smile which is always there. She is forever young which might be why she can never seem to stay in one place for long. Her laugh is the most wonderful sound, which she shares openly and freely. She is able to shape shift. Syd and Echo haven't seen her shift, but they have noticed glimmers of the possibility in her eyes and voice depending on what their discussion was during their online meetings.

Syd and Raven recognize each other instantly, exchanging looks as they are waiting at the baggage carousels. They walk out to the curb separately, quietly trying to blend in with the other tourists, not wanting to draw attention to themselves just in case they are being watched or followed. They had created their plans together during their secret meetings online over the past few months discussing every possibility to ensure success on their very first mission.

Misty is usually somewhere around watching, protecting, listening; however, Echo can't seem to locate her. She had hoped Misty would show up in Cancun. Echo pulls up to the curb, and they both jump in as they all begin talking at once. They have so much to say to each other, lifetimes of stored up memories to share. Knowing they have to complete this journey first and then hopefully relax enough to enjoy their reunion. Echo tells them she has rented a beach house just outside of Cancun. "We can spend the night there after we retrieve the first skull, this will give us some much-needed time to plan for the next journey."

"Wow, the four cosmic sisters finally together in person," Syd says quietly. "We need to know how and where to locate all the rest of the skulls, but most importantly, what are we to do with them once they are all safely in our possession?"

"One moment at a time," Raven says with that glorious smile of hers.

"All right, ladies, I need to take a look at the map first. I have a feeling about where we should go, but I want to be sure." Syd looks around trying to get her bearings.

"The map is there on the seat. I have the ruins circled and highlighted along with the best route to each one," Echo tells her.

"I see it, we are going to El Meco. Head north on Tulum/México 307 for about 25 kilos," Syd exclaims excitedly.

"Tell us all you know, Syd," Raven chimes in as Echo pulls out onto the highway.

With a deep sigh, Syd shares her story: "I

only have flashes of memories, so it's hard sometimes for me to make sense of them; especially since many of the places that were villages back then are now ruins. They look very different. Looking at the map helps some, but we won't know for sure until we get there. I know it was hidden during a time when the Mayan people lived here. History books say El Meco was abandoned around 600 AD and has remained virtually untouched since then. My guess is since the majority of tourists take guided tours that all lead to larger ruin sites, Meco has been overlooked. There are no guided tours there, so we should be able to scout about freely, I am pretty sure this is the place."

As they drive along the beautiful coastal road, they catch glimpses of the ocean through the lush trees and flowers. It is spring time here in Mexico; the flowers are blooming everywhere and the smell of the ocean breezes carry in scents of salty air mixed with a sweetness from the flowers.

Echo always feels energized when she is near the Caribbean. It is where she feels the most connected to Source. As if her soul came from the sea. The energy level between the sisters is at an all-time high now that they are physically together. There is no need for words as they turn their focus to finding the first skull as quickly as possible. Echo knows they are not being followed—that is one thing she is positive of—as she checks her rearview mirror. Even so, she still has the unshakable feeling that something is off.

Misty still hasn't shown up. Echo is not sure why, but her mind begins to wander again. She thinks to herself, *I must stay focused on getting us to the ruins and getting the skull safely out of there. Then we can figure out what happened to Misty. We sisters agreed long ago that saving the skulls is our highest priority.* And she returns her focus to driving.

CHAPTER 4

Captain Jim announces over the jet speaker: "Mr. Axler, we will be landing in five minutes, Sir."

Mr. Axler checks his watch as he folds the maps and returns them to his briefcase. He sends a text to his driver, Miguel, who better be waiting at the airport to take him to his hotel.

Hola, Señor *Axler, I am parked and waiting,* Miguel replies immediately.

This new pilot is one of the best in the world, Mr. Axler thinks as he looks out the window of his Gulfstream. *I was lucky to find him.* He smiles to himself as Captain Jim executes a perfect landing.

Climbing down the stairs into the Caribbean sunshine, Mr. Axler spots a car and, just as he expected, Miguel is waiting for him. Having your own plane definitely has its advantages. Mr. Axler glances at his wrist again; he sees no other messages. He is happy to see that as it will give him time to shower and nap before his meeting with his team.

"No luggage, Señor?" asks Miguel.

"Not this trip; I will be leaving this evening. I will let you know later what time to pick me up. Right now I need you to drop me off at the Grand Fiesta, rapido," Mr. Axler says gruffly as he climbs into the back of the black Sedan.

⁂

AS THE SISTERS PULL OFF INTO THE ENTRANCE to El Meco, they are relieved to see that the parking lot is empty.

Raven says, "Echo, stop here, and I will go close the gate to the entrance. That way if anyone does show up, they will think it is closed for the day."

They park the SUV at the far end of the park to remain hidden from the front entrance.

"I picked up some tools; they're in the large duffle bag," Echo tells them. "There is water and snacks in the back as well."

"I don't think we need any tools today. I feel the skull's energy already," Syd says, handing Echo and Raven each a water bottle. Syd turns and starts walking up the trail. She seems robotic in her movements.

Following behind her, Echo looks over at Raven and asks, "You feel it, too?"

They begin climbing the steps behind Syd as she appears to know exactly where to go. Syd stops midway up and moves off the stairs onto a rocky pathway. Raven and Echo exchange another look because Syd appears to be in some kind of trance.

"Reveal to me, Pacal the Great, the secrets you keep. Show me the gate," Syd is whispering over and over in a voice that sounds as old as time, moving slowly along this narrow pathway, running her hands along the ancient stone wall. Suddenly, there is a brief shimmer as the stones fade away, revealing a small opening into the pyramid. Echo and Raven continue to follow Syd into the cool, stone structure. Raven switches on a flashlight she must have grabbed from the duffle bag. Echo reaches up to grab hold of Raven's shoulder. Raven looks back and smiles. Echo feels the warmth radiating from Raven; her love literally vibrates throughout her body as they continue deeper into the pyramid.

The energy inside the pyramid is so powerful Raven and Echo have to stop for a moment to catch their breath. However, Syd doesn't seem to notice as she continues walking, turning off just ahead of them. They hurry to catch up. Syd has entered a very small room which feels suffocating like a dry sauna.

Echo stands still, attempting to slow down her breathing, and takes off her pack to lay it down, never taking her eyes off of Syd. Syd is still whispering, but Echo is unable to understand what language she is using now.

Suddenly, Syd stops at the far back wall; Raven and Echo move in behind her, and they see hieroglyphics written onto the walls. Syd is still whispering, but they realize she is actually reading what is written there. Raven and Echo exchange another surprised look, while Raven shines the light onto the symbols. Syd continues to whisper, waving her hand over the largest stone with odd markings which look slightly different from all the other ones. Once again, they catch a brief shimmer before the stone disappears.

Echo steps forward as she catches the sparkle of a small crystal skull sitting behind it. She whispers to herself, "Could it be that simple?" In that instant, she feels as if this skull is pulling her into it, she is not able to stop herself.

Echo reaches out to take the skull almost against her will and, just as her hand touches it, she hears Syd screaming, "NOOOOOOOO!"

Echo is slammed back and lands hard on the ground. She tries to hold onto the skull for fear of it breaking, but the skull rolls away from her. She is badly shaken and lays there on the ground stunned. She looks around the tomb which looks the same except now she is alone. The tomb is completely quiet aside from an awful gasping sound. It takes Echo a moment to realize those sounds are coming from her. She continues to lay there on the dirt floor, trying to figure out what just happened.

Where are Raven and Syd?

After a few more moments, Echo feels like she can stand up. She looks up at the wall; the opening is gone; it has returned to the original stone but there are no markings. She is left in darkness, except for a slight glow coming from the skull. Afraid to touch it again, she needs to figure out what just happened.

Echo calls out, "Syd? Raven? Mmmmisty?" in a voice that does not even sound like hers. On shaky legs, she feels her way along the walls until she finds the opening. She is so grateful it is still there as she steps outside into darkness with only a sliver of moonlight to light her way.

The stones look new, the musty smell gone. The jungle looks different—scary, more lush. She has an overwhelming sense of deja vu. Feeling disoriented, she is not able figure out what time it is, which is odd for her. She knows it was early when they arrived in Cancun. They drove straight over to the ruins, so, by her calculations, it should be about 11 am. Her mind and heart are racing; she knows she didn't alter or bend time.

So how could it be evening and fairly late? she thinks as she looks up to see the sliver of moon high in the sky. She begins trying to figure this out. She looks around, pretty sure she is in the same ruins, but not exactly the ones they entered this morning. Clearly, Syd and Raven are not there with her. She knows they would have answered her by now, and her radar has gone completely quiet. As a matter of fact, she doesn't feel anyone she loves at all. "Misty?" she whispers again to the night, hoping, waiting. Nothing.

Echo can feel energy coming from the skull but it is odd—more like a humming sound, very low, vibrational humming, like the ohmmmm sound she makes sometimes in her meditations. She continues to feel the skull pulling her, calling to her somehow. Echo looks over at the skull and says, "No way, skull. I am not about to touch you again."

She decides she had better go back inside the pyramid just in case anyone (or thing) shows up tonight. She does not return to the room with the skull even though she still feels it calling to her.

Sitting down against the wall just inside the opening, Echo decides to wait until morning light to investigate. Hopefully, she will be able to figure this out, get back her bearings—her sense of time. She thinks, *Maybe, just maybe, in the daylight, I can find a clue as to where I am.*

She sits there in the dark just beyond the moonlight for the longest time, trying to hear something other than the skull humming. It is so eerily quiet. No other sounds; nothing to help her figure out what is going on.

She falls asleep, dreaming of times past, searching for something she has lost. She can not remember what it is, she is walking through a thick foggy mist, with no concept of time or space. Feeling such a void of everything living until she is jolted awake by a tsunami of memories past—or maybe future—racing around in her brain, overflowing, overwhelming her. She reaches out her hand, her body is shaking, again, she hears awful, raspy, gasping breaths and realizes they are hers. She begins feeling around her, searching for her backpack, wanting to write down the dreams. That always helps her make sense of all the information flowing to her. Oh, rats—she remembers now—she took it off in the tomb.

Wide awake now, "Oh no! This is not good, without my pack I have no water or food," she exclaims.

Feeling shaken, lost, and so unsure of what has happened, Echo stands up and leans against the cool stones. *At least it is daylight now,* she thinks. *I am in the ruins, but where in time did I land? I am not sure that this is even real, this place is void of sound, except that annoying, vibrating skull.*

The place feels so empty, cold, even though she is in Mexico. Echo can see the sun is just peeking out above the horizon as she heads down the steps to explore. She can easily see now that she is in exactly in the same place, but a very different time. The stones on the pyramid and steps are not worn away. The path is actually a clear, worn, dirt path. There were fallen stones covering it when she and her sisters were on it.

As Echo continues down the steps, looking around, she sees a village. Yet, the village is completely abandoned—not one living thing at all. It looks as if whoever did live here left in a big hurry. All of their belongings strewn about the ruins, which aren't really ruins now. They are full buildings and pathways as she can now see as she continues looking around. The parking lot is gone and now fire pits, grass-type mats, clay pots, and small huts are in its place. A small village, yet so void of feeling, so incredibly silent.

There are no sounds, no birds chirping, nothing, not a sound coming from the jungle or distant ocean, not even a breeze. It is as if they just disappeared in an instant, all living things except the thick jungle brush and trees surrounding the ruins. Echo is not sure the jungle is really there or if it is just an illusion, and she is not about to investigate any further. That is one adventure she plans to skip.

She starts searching among the little village for something she could use to gather up the odd little crystal skull. She thinks this can not be the skull they were searching for—it must be a time gate or something. Echo has a feeling she needs to place the skull back in the original place, although she is not exactly sure why. She just knows she must. Perhaps it might help her to return to her own time and place.

Elated she could find a clay pot that isn't cracked and has a lid, Echo picks up a large stick and heads back into the pyramid. Using the stick, she pushes the skull gently into the clay pot and covers it. Echo lets out a very large sigh, realizing she was holding her breath the entire time. She lifts the pot, praying that it will not take her somewhere else. She takes several deep breaths as she carries it over to the large stones.

"I hope I can remember how Syd opened that holographic rock," she says to herself. Echo stops in her tracks and looks all round; she can not find any markings to show her which stone it was. She is searching her brain, trying to remember the words Syd whispered, and if she made the markings appear with her words or if they were already there.

All of a sudden, she hears footsteps, which sound eerily loud in the silence of this non-place. Echo nearly jumps out of her skin, pulling the pot tightly to her body and slides behind a large woven mat leaning against the wall. She peeks through the palms as Syd enters the room!

Echo immediately knows this is not the Syd she just met. This Syd is different; she moves as if she is gliding, floating almost. She is slightly taller, very thin, with longer limbs and her skin almost glows. It looks like it is made of a metallic liquid, somewhat like mercury. She watches her move to the corner and begin drawing on the rocks with some type of tool.

The tool cuts right through the stone as if it was butter, but it makes no sound at all.

This glowing Syd is carving out hieroglyphic images onto the stones, and when she is finished, she begins to carve out a triangular shape at the very base of the stones. Echo remains frozen behind the mat, barely breathing. She is not sure what might happen if Syd sees her, or if she even *could* see her. Echo still isn't even sure if this is real—maybe she is still dreaming. She thinks to herself, *It doesn't matter because I am not about to find out,* as she remains hidden behind the mat watching.

Syd finishes the carving, and Echo cannot see the tool any longer. Syd now has a pyramid-shaped object in her hands, which looks like it is made out of the same metallics that covers Syd, although it looks more solid. Syd places it into the hole she had carved out of the stone, waves her hands, and the wall becomes solid again.

The room begins to heat up; Echo feels it radiating from the wall. She feels a big energy shift—a vibrating electric feeling—and finds it difficult to stay still, hidden behind the mat. Echo feels as if her energy is being drained right out of her as Syd glides out of the room.

Oddly enough, Echo does not hear footsteps this time.

Echo steps out from behind the mat and slowly walks back to the entrance. She stops just before the opening and listens for the other Syd. No sounds at all, just the odd quiet non-place feeling. Echo returns to the skull room, searching the wall again, hoping to find the correct marking the fake skull was hiding behind.

Holding the clay pot close to her body, Echo lays her other hand on the rock, trying to remember the words Syd whispered. She feels the stone disappear before her and carefully slides the pot back onto the shelf, holding her breath again as she lets go. Thankfully, it stays there as she watches the stone return to cover the hiding spot.

Echo feels weak as she walks back outside on very shaky legs. She knows she must figure out how to return to her time, but she needs a moment to process what just happened. She believes she was sent back in time by touching the skull. A very long, long time ago because the ruins are not ruins—they are a village now, and she remembers Syd mentioning something about a village of the past. Although she really isn't sure of anything right now.

Echo sits down in the sunshine, knowing she better figure this out quickly. "Let's see," she says quietly, "I am going to need to be very careful when I go forward. I don't want to get confused. I have never bent this much time before, and I am not sure what time period I am even in."

Feeling like she is losing herself in this non-place, it is imperative she gets out of here as soon as possible. This place does not feel real, as if there is no Earth's polarity here; some sort of black hole; possibly another universe. Echo is struggling to figure it out, trying to remember all she learned about the Mayan ruins. What time period did they exist in?

"Oh, Misty, where are you?" she says out loud.

She remembers her teaching from Misty: "Echo, you can't think your way out, you must *feel* your way through time."

She slowly lowers herself into a lotus pose, meditating, calming her racing mind, slowing down her breathing. One thing is for certain: she knows she can't move freely about time if she's in a state of anxiety. As her mind continues to clear, she sees in her mind's eye Misty teaching her long, long ago, telling her how to connect soul, body, and mind, how to use the connection with Earth. Allowing Source energy to flow to her and through her. Breathing, feeling the universe flowing through her body, she can still hear the skull humming. It seems to be growing louder, mixing with the other skulls' energy, Echo can feel all the vibrations joining together.

"How interesting," she whispers as she feels the skulls, the energy of Source all connecting her to this place. As if she is a part of the ruins, she sees the history unfolding in her mind just as if she is watching a movie.

In her mind's eye, she sees the Mayan people moving about in their little village, feels how beautiful, peaceful, and loving this tribe is, and then they are gone, vanished. Almost simultaneously, she feels herself moving forward through time; the pyramids begin to age; the village has faded away. She sees Syd and Raven searching for her, calling out to her, asking for Misty to help. Echo answers back, "I am here! I am here!" but they can not hear her.

She continues mediating, her body aching, telling her a long, long time has passed. As the sun begins to sink, Echo feels uneasy. She does not trust anything here in this place with no sound or life. She feels the *ohmmmmmm* sound from the skulls; this has to be the key, but how?

Feeling completely drained of physical energy, Echo drifts off into another dream. She is floating along with Misty, listening to her whisper, "Echo, you must not *bend* time. You must *become* time. You have to collapse it so you can just step through like a veil."

Echo attempts to ask her how, but she is jolted awake as she feels like she has fallen off a cliff. She is still seated on the ground. Realizing she must have fallen asleep, she reminds herself to breathe in, breathe out . . . deeply. And she begins to meditate again.

This time she hums, matching her voice to the low vibrations of the skull's humming, allowing pictures of this village turning to ruins to float through her mind again. Echo imagines a veil surrounding it, then pictures the veil folding over and back, like one of those paper fans she used to make when she was a little girl. As she holds that vision, she creates a space in the veil, one just her size, so she can step into it just as Misty instructed.

Self-doubt creeps in the back of her mind, and, just like that, the vision is gone in an instant. "Good grief!" Echo cries out loud in frustration. "I have not had thoughts of self-doubt since I was young! It must be this NON-place."

Feeling so lost, unsure of what happened to her, she knows she must rise above this void and trust herself. Something that has always brought her peace, joy, a complete love for all, besides yoga and meditation, is moving her body to music. Knowing she must escape this place right now, or possibly be lost forever, Echo stands up, stretches, and begins to dance while singing her favorite songs. She has a hard time remembering all the words, which makes her laugh.

Ooohhhhh, there is my joy. Yes, she thinks.

Echo begins to sing out loud, "Off to see the lizard, deja deja deja vu," staying in tune with the low drumming-type frequency the skulls are humming, dancing around while she imagines all the instruments playing. Echo is laughing out loud, feeling the joy, the love, and allowing it to fill her completely. She pictures the veil she created as it begins to float and fold itself.

"Yes," she says, laughing as she continues to imagine the music playing.

A space begins to open inside the veil and *BAM!* She feels the shift immediately as she once again lands on the ground hard. She is laughing so hard tears are running down her cheeks. "Yes, I have never been so happy in my life!" she shouts.

Echo lies on the ground just outside of a ruined pyramid, gazing up into a star-filled, dark sky, hearing sweet, normal, beautiful sounds. She feels the ocean breeze tickle her skin as she breathes in the salty air. Once again, tears of sheer joy begin to stream down her face.

"Misty, are you here?" Echo calls out a few times in a whisper. Standing up on wobbly legs, she walks over to the ruins and sits against the wall of stones. She sighs, feeling the cool stones on her back, the earth solid beneath her, sounds —sweet, sweet sounds—finally.

Still feeling somewhat disoriented, Echo is not sure how long she was gone, but she is positive she has returned to the right place and time. Sitting alone in the ruins, Echo drifts off to a peaceful sleep, listening to the wonderful sounds, enjoying a cool, ocean breeze. Full of gratitude.

Just before dawn, Echo is startled awake by whispering voices as she sees a young couple climbing the steps to the ruined pyramid. She doesn't want to scare them, so she inches around the side of the wall, thinking as soon as they pass by, she can escape unnoticed.

"Are you sure this is it?" a young girl whispers to the man.

"YES. I was given specific instructions. Follow me. I know what to look for. Now stop asking me so many questions," the boy answers, his voice getting louder.

Echo chances a peek around the corner just as he is climbing over the steps in exactly the same place Syd climbed.

"Did you bring the case I told you to find?" he asks.

"Of course, I did. It took me a while to get the exact one you described. Now will you finally explain to me exactly what we are going to do once we find this skull?"

"Shhhh! I told you to stop talking about it," he says angrily.

Echo peeks again as she sees the girl

following him into the ruins, carrying a small, very old suitcase—one that looks like the old-time doctor bags you see in black-and-white movies. Echo decides in that instant to stay put, out of sight. She realizes she does not have enough information on the crystal skull or how Syd had planned to remove it, or what even happened to Syd and Raven after she disappeared to the non-place. After all she has experienced, Echo is feeling somewhat disoriented, not at all sure she has enough energy to blend or hide to follow them into the pyramid.

She sits and waits as the sun rises higher in the sky, realizing she desperately needs some water. Echo decides to climb down, pretending to be a tourist out for a stroll. She is weak, and her legs feel as wobbly as a newborn colt's.

Oh, I really need something to eat. And a shower and a soft bed would be fabulous, she muses to herself. Echo winds her way around to the main path, stopping at the historical markers, trying to blend in as a few other tourists begin to arrive.

She continues to move around the markers, looking for the young couple to return. As the few visitors leave, Echo climbs the stairs once again. After one last look around to make sure she is alone, she heads over the stones to the same path she took with Syd and Raven, but the door is gone. "Hmmm, I didn't see them leave. . ." she says in a whisper to herself.

Echo wishes Misty would eventually show up as she sure could use her help. She can't shake the feeling that something has happened to Misty.

CHAPTER 5

Raven, Syd, and Echo had agreed to book rooms at different hotels just in case something went wrong. Echo remembers Raven booked one right by the airport. Thinking that would be where Raven and Syd would have gone for the night, she decides she would try to find a ride there. She continues strolling along the paths, still feel uneasy. Everything looks the same, yet it just feels off. Echo stops a moment and checks in with her radar, realizing it is completely quiet, and her body begins to shiver. Such an odd feeling, no wonder they have not returned to look for her.

She realizes how exhausted she is, as well as

very thirsty and hungry. She sees an older couple walking along the path.

"Hi, I was wondering if you could help me? I got separated from my group and need to get back into town to the hotel. Would you be able to give me a ride?" Echo asks them; her voice doesn't even sound like it belongs to her.

"Yes, we would be happy to," the older man says as he reaches his hand out. "I'm Thomas, this is my wife, Gracie. Where are you staying?"

"I'm, I'm Mary. Thank you so much for helping me. I'm staying near the airport— Hampton Inn," Echo stammers as she shakes his hand.

"Hmmmm," Thomas said. "Never heard of it, but that doesn't mean anything. This is our first trip to Mexico. I am sure we can find it. Come on, let's go, the afternoons here are wicked, and you, Dearie, look a bit off color. We have some water in the car."

"Thank you! I got separated from my group and finally found my way here this morning," Echo tells him, trying to appear as normal as possible while following them to the parking lot. She thinks, *I doubt very much they would want to take me anywhere if I said,*

'Hey, I'm Echo. I am saving the world but got lost in time, and now we may die if I don't find my way back.'

"Thank you so much for the water. Where did you say you were from?" she asks them after downing the entire bottle.

"We're from Burford, England. This is our first trip to Mexico," Gracie said quietly. "We are staying near the airport, too. I'm glad we can help. I sure hope you find your friends."

"Me too!" Oh, if they only knew how much. Feeling exhausted, wishing they could get there without all the chatting, she gathers her strength as she knows it is absolutely necessary to appear as normal as she can, given the situation. "How long are you staying?"

"Oh, we are planning to spend a month or more exploring. We are starting in Mexico and then plan to go north to the US. Where are you from?" Gracie asks.

"Uh, Dallas, Texas. I hope you get a chance to stop and check it out," Echo replies, trying desperately to keep her eyes open. She thinks, *What I really need is a hot shower, some strong coffee, or a very long nap,* as she gazes out the window. She still has the feeling something is just not right, but what? Maybe it's the exhaustion and lack of food.

"Mary! Mary! Oh, Mary, wake up!" Gracie says as she gently shakes Echo. Echo jumps awake, completely startled.

"I'm sorry, I didn't mean to fall asleep. Where are we?" she says, looking around. Nothing looks familiar at all, and she wonders how long was she out.

"You told us you were staying at a hotel across from the airport, right? Well, this is the only one there is—" Thomas says as Gracie interrupts.

"—Hampton Inn, isn't that what you called it, Mary? We couldn't find any hotel with that name anywhere in Mexico. Are you sure you're feeling all right, Honey?"

"Oh my, I must have been more tired than I thought. This is it, the uhm—" she says, looking around for a sign, "Grand Fiesta. Yes, Ma'am, this is it. Thank you so much!" Echo tells them while jumping out of the back of their car. "Have a wonderful trip, Y'all."

Without looking back, Echo enters the lobby with her mind racing. *I know there was a Hampton Inn here, we passed it on our way out to the ruins this morning.* Now she knows she is not in the right time and decides she better get somewhere safe. *Oh, shoot, how am I going to get a room without my wallet? It's in my backpack. I have no passport, no credit cards, no money. This is not a good situation,* she thinks as she looks around the lobby. "Oh, Misty, where on Earth are you?" she whispers.

Where have I traveled to? Echo thinks feeling confused and weak again. She spots the bathroom doors to her right in a hallway off the lobby. She quickly moves into the bathroom and begins deep breathing, trying to pull herself together. She decides to at least wash her face, and when she looks up in the mirror, she is startled. Echo thinks, *I can't believe they gave me a ride looking like this. What a hot mess, seriously, Girl, pull yourself together!*

She continues washing her face the best she can, attempts to tame her wild hair, and brushes her clothes off while trying to figure out a plan. She takes a few more cleansing breaths to calm herself. "All right, I can figure this out," Echo says to her reflection in the mirror. *It must be close to checkout time,* she thinks as she exits the bathroom and finds the stairwell.

Echo climbs the stairs to the top floor. She

spots the maids' cleaning cart and peeks into the trash, hoping for a newspaper. No luck. She hears the cleaning crew coming out of the room in front of the cart. Echo leans back into the wall, centering herself with slow, deep breaths. She closes her eyes and sets her intention to have enough energy to bend time. She just needs a few seconds to grab the door before it closes so she can sneak in unseen.

She makes it into the room, feeling completely drained of all energy. Echo can barely hold herself up right now, unsure of what she needs most: sleep, food, or a shower. *Maybe all of the above*, she thinks. *I will sit down on the bed for a moment and decide.*

Sleep is all she can think of. Thankfully, there is an alarm clock in the room. She sets the alarm to go off in one hour. Echo lays back onto the bed and immediately falls into a deep, deep sleep, her last thoughts creating a protection incantation to prevent anyone from entering the room.

CHAPTER 6

The alarm wakes her just as she feels like someone is pushing her out of bed. She was in a very dark place—a different dimension from a long time ago. Echo was battling a force that had taken over Misty when Misty was in a human form. Echo's dreams were speaking to her again. She searches the room for her backpack and remembers she doesn't have it with her.

She is fully alert now as she remembers she must find the way back to her timeline. Echo decides a quick shower will help. "This feels like heaven," she thinks as the warm water washes the dirt off.

She wonders how much time must have

K.J. KING

passed for her to be so full of dirt. If feels as if she only just touched that skull, and yet her body and empty stomach remind her it must have been days. As she rinses the shampoo from her long, blonde hair, she thinks to herself, *Time has always been my one constant along with my internal radar—I have always known what time it was. Now, not only do I not even know what day it is, I have no idea where I am. I do know it is not my world.*

Feeling better now that she slept and had a hot shower, Echo looks at her clothes, hating to put them back on and wrinkling her nose at the musty smell, she reluctantly gets dressed. She shrugs her shoulders, thinking, *At least I showered.*

Turning on the TV in hopes of seeing the news or something that will give her an indication of where she is in time, she towel-dries her hair. Discovering that today's date is the same as when they first arrived in Mexico, but it can't possibly be the same universe, she thinks, *All I have to do is find my universe . . . like that's going to be easy.*

Echo sighs. Pacing the floor, she attempts to figure out a plan. Without identification or money she realizes she will have to be very creative. Her mind racing once again, knowing it will block her from her gifts, she immediately sits down lotus style to meditate and center herself to allow complete peace to envelope her. Her mind quiets, and she connects with Source.

"I know this is the answer. I just let my human-ness run away with me sometimes," she whispers.

Once again, she begins to see the ruins she visited with her sisters, allowing the veil of time to unfold, searching for Raven and Syd.

The door to her room flies open, and before she even sees who has entered, Echo reverses time just enough to slip out of the hotel room unnoticed. As she dashes down the hallway and turns the corner, she glances back quickly just to make sure she was not seen.

"Stop right there," shouts a female voice. Echo turns to see the same girl from the ruins with her hands raised, holding what looks like a laser pointer right at Echo's chest. Echo takes a deep breath in as she attempts to shift time.

Echo is instantly back in the same room but she is sitting in a chair. She hears the couple from the ruins whispering. She realizes she feels very strange. Actually, it is that she can not feel at all which is the oddest feeling ever, nor can she move anything. What is happening?

"I know you're awake now," the man tells Echo without turning around.

Echo keeps her eyes closed trying very hard to shift time, stopping abruptly when she realizes that without a connection to her body, she could end up shifting right out of her Earthly form. Fear grips her entire being. Real fear, not the kind when you feel startled. The life-flashing-before-your-eyes kind of fear. As she realizes if she shifted time without a body, she could end up like Misty, or worse, end up in the non-place forever. Her very next thought is, *It doesn't matter, because if I don't find all the skulls, we might not have a planet to live on, anyway.*

The man grabs Echo's hair, lifting her head up roughly. "I said I know you're awake. I need answers."

Echo slowly opens her eyes. It takes great concentration to make them open. The man and woman are standing there staring at her. She feels as if they know who she is.

"I don't know what you're talking about," Echo attempts to say. Her mouth is numb, and again it takes great effort to move.

"We know you're a time traveler, Echo. We know you seek the skull. We have searched your room; it isn't here, you either hid it or didn't find it. WHICH IS IT?" he yells into Echo's face. The girl stands next to him pointing that laser thingy at her.

"Skull? I have no idea what——" Echo tries to say, but he cuts her off.

"TELL ME NOW OR I WILL MAKE YOU!"

Before Echo can make a sound, she feels as if his hands are inside her head, squeezing her brain. The pressure is unbearable. Echo hears screams and realizes they are coming from her.

The pain stops suddenly. "Okay! Okay! Okay!" she gasps. "I didn't find it——"

He cuts her off again. "YOU LIE! TELL ME WHERE IT IS!" As the searing pressure inside her head starts again, it feels as if her brain is now on fire.

"The ruins," Echo's words are barely heard over her gasps for breath.

He moves to the door, opens it, then looks back at Echo and the girl. The girl steps forward, and in one swift move, throws Echo over her shoulder like a sack of potatoes. They all go down the stairs, out a side door of the hotel into the blinding hot sun.

Echo has to close her eyes as she can't adjust to the brightness. She attempts some deep breathing, meditating to try to reconnect herself and remain calm. There is something preventing her from connecting her mind to her body. She can't figure out what has happened. She knows she is in her body because she can see it, but she can't move or feel anything below her neck. It is as if she is trapped inside her headspace.

The girl literally tosses Echo onto the back seat as if Echo weighs nothing at all. Echo attempts to sit up but can't and looks down at her body to see if she is tied. Her body looks normal, but no matter how hard she tries, she can't move. Echo focuses all her energy on listening, it is all she has right now. She can hear the sounds of traffic, and, looking up, she sees the sky and an occasional building, but nothing to help her out of this mess. Then a phone rings.

The girl answers, "Yes, Sir, this is Pepper."

Echo can hear a male voice speaking to Pepper but cannot quite hear what he is saying.

"We do, yes. I'll call you once we have it," Pepper said.

Echo attempts to turn her head to hear better, but just the movement makes her completely dizzy. As she passes out, she whispers, "Help."

CHAPTER 7

"Open your mouth," Pepper says as she holds a bottle of water with one hand and Echo's chin with the other. Echo does and is surprised that she can move her mouth, and it doesn't feel numb. *I hope that's water she's giving me. It tastes like water, and I do feel better,* Echo thinks. Her eyes are able to adjust to the bright sunlight now, and she notices that tears are running down her face. *I wasn't even aware I had been crying,* Echo thinks as she looks around, realizing Pepper has carried her back to the ruins.

Pepper lifts Echo up onto her feet, leaning her against the wall and placing the water bottle into her hand, but the bottle falls as Echo can't grasp it. Pepper never takes her eyes off Echo as she bends over to pick up the water bottle.

"Open," Pepper says grabbing Echo's chin once again.

Echo drinks greedily just like a newborn baby bird. She is surprised and relieved as she can feel the cool water going down into her stomach.

"Okay, where is it?" the man asks impatiently.

Pepper grabs Echo's arm and begins walking. Echo is shocked that her body follows along like a puppet, stumbling along the path behind the girl—Pepper. Echo searches her memory; she still doesn't feel fully together but at least she is moving again. Trying to remember exactly what Syd had done to open the stones to the fake skull.

The walking is helping her feel whole, connected again. Echo, lost in thought, stumbles and falls forward right into Pepper. Pepper grabs hold of Echo and prevents them from hitting the ground together. As she helps Echo stand, they lock eyes. Echo can feel the compassion and realizes this girl does not intend to hurt her.

"Thank you," Echo says quietly.

Pepper lets go of her and turns back toward the narrow pathway. Echo continues standing there, slowing her breathing, allowing inner peace and calm to flood her mind, body, and soul. A memory pops into her head. It's of Misty's soothing voice: "Echo, you must not bend time, you must become it. Collapse it so you can just step through the veil. Feel where you want to be in time." Echo breathes in a slow long breath, feeling her sister's love surrounding her, allowing her mind to quiet and become clear.

She can feel the man's anger, concerned he will play his Jedi mind tricks on her again, she almost laughs out loud at the thought. Shaking her head, she smiles to herself, remembering all the sci-fi movies she watched when she was little. Echo allows the thoughts to pass. *Stay in your peace,* she silently tells herself.

Echo moves quickly to catch up to the couple as they enter the tiny room. She continues deep breathing in and out, completely clearing her mind of all thoughts, then begins to soften her vision, focusing on the veil she sees unfolding before her.

"Find it!" the man says gruffly to Echo.

She walks over to the wall and places her hands over the markings, whispering the same words that Syd said; however, she has no idea how. The stone once again shimmers, disappears, and there is the old Mayan pot just as she had left it. "I hid the skull inside this pot," Echo says, reaching for it.

She carefully turns and hands the pot to the man. As he takes the pot from Echo, she takes a deep breath and steps backward into the veil, allowing all the love she shares with her sisters to fill every cell in her body, a love so pure it flows from your soul, from Source energy. Feeling the indescribable connection to Source, to the earth, all things living, she pictures her sisters. *Bam*, she is thrown to the ground again, but this time she is there with them.

She hears her sisters calling to her, and she realizes she must have passed out again, because this time she hears Syd not in her mind but in person. "Echo! Echo, wake up, please!"

CHAPTER 8

As Echo opens her eyes, she sees Syd and Raven standing over her looking very concerned.

"Where are we? What time is it?" Echo asks urgently.

"We're in the ruins. Echo, are you okay?" Raven asks as she rummages in her pack for a bottle of water. "Here, drink this, you passed out."

"Thank you," Echo says as she attempts to take the bottle, but her hands are shaking so much she can't. Raven helps Echo drink. "Oh, my gosh, I swear this is the best water I have ever had in my entire life," Echo says after she gulps the entire bottle down.

"What happened?" Syd asks, sitting down next to her sisters.

"I don't have time to explain, did you find what we came for?" Echo asks.

Syd shakes her head "No. Not the one we need. I am afraid that is a replica." She points to the large stone.

"YES! Yes it is," Echo says, realizing that she has returned to the moment just before she touched that odd skull this morning. "I know where it is! Help me up," Echo exclaims as she reaches for Raven's hand.

Syd jumps up and grabs Echo's other hand and they both help her stand. Echo squeezes their hands as they pull her to stand, pausing for a moment, smiling, appreciating the deep love they share with each other that feels even more precious to Echo after what she just went through.

Echo leads them over to the far corner of the room where she says, "Syd, if you will place your hands here, the markings will reveal themselves, and you will know what to do."

Turning to face Raven, Echo tells her, "Raven, grab my backpack, please. I brought a case to put the skull in. I have a feeling you and I can't touch them, but I know Syd can."

Raven looks at Echo with raised eyebrows and knows exactly what Echo is thinking. But the story will have to wait; they need to get out of there as quickly as they can. Echo is concerned that the couple, or whoever sent them, may be able to follow them. She doubts it will take them long to discover the other skull is a fake, unless they touch it, and it takes them to the non-place. Honestly, she hopes they do not, she wouldn't want anyone to end up in that place. Echo's entire body shivers at the thought as she turns back to watch Syd.

Syd find the markings; she is moving as if in a trance again. Syd begins whispering, and Echo catches a glimpse of the metallic pyramid she saw Syd put there so long ago. Warm energy floods the room, and the vibrations increase again—a humming ohm sound as Syd lifts the skull and places it into the container Echo brought.

They are all very quiet as they leave the pyramid and head over to the car. Echo, feeling more alert now than ever, looks around thinking,

I didn't realize others would be looking for the skulls, I knew to watch out for the empty faces. Wow, I was so wrong. She feels anxious to share her story with Syd and Raven. They might know who this couple was, but that story will have to wait.

"Okay, I don't have time to explain, but just trust me, please! Raven, will you figure out somewhere we can go? We can't go to any of the hotels we booked. The map is on the back seat if you need it," Echo says, starting the car. She turns to look behind her and sees Syd in the back seat with a very blank look on her face. "Syd, you okay?"

"Yes, I think so, just feeling a bit wonky," Syd says slowly, sounding a bit tipsy.

Echo pulls out of the parking lot onto the main road and begins laughing uncontrollably. Raven and Syd join in, and soon they are all laughing and crying at the same time.

Raven points to her left, laughing so hard she is unable to form words. Echo turns the car left, driving toward Playa del Carmen, not sure where they are going, not that she cares. Right now she feels safe and is with her sisters again. She is enjoying every moment.

As they drive along the long stretch of road, Echo notices the clear blue sky, she can smell ocean, and she feels so relaxed to be back in her world. The car is quiet, each sister lost in her own thoughts. Echo begins to wonder how long she has been gone, it is hard to tell, but her body knows. As she relaxes, her body begins to let her know she has been gone a while; her stomach begins to grumble and the loudest sound ever escapes—sounding like she has a mountain lion inside of her.

Raven turns quickly to look at Echo, "What in the world, Echo?"

"Wow! I guess I need to eat something," Echo, still laughing, holds her stomach.

Raven rolls her eyes at her, "I thought you might be shifting into a lioness."

"Nope! That's your thang, sister! Since you know where we're going, is there some place we can stop and eat? Like NOW?" Echo replies in her deepest southern accent.

"Yes, as a matter of fact, I have a friend whose grandparents live just outside of Aduana, which is where we are heading," Raven says, still smiling.

Just as Echo was beginning to wonder if Raven knew where she was going, she catches a whiff of the most delightful mixture of spices, and, there in the distance, she sees a tiny little shack out in the middle of nowhere.

"We're here!" Raven says, pointing at the tiny home. They pull onto the drive as a petite woman steps out onto the porch.

"Mija, Que gusto en verte!" she shouts, walking toward them waving her arms. The biggest smile on her lovely brown face.

"Hola, Abuela!" Raven yells back as she jumps out, running over to her, gently pulling her into a bear hug. Syd and Echo stand waiting for them to finish their embrace that feels like an eternity. Echo's stomach lets out another terrible loud roar.

"Oh mi ven a comer," Grandma says as she shoos them all inside.

Grandpa is already setting the table. The smells coming from the kitchen are amazing. Echo spies chips, salsa, and guacamole. "We have arrived in Nirvana," she says, feeling as if they knew she hadn't eaten in days.

Pepper sends a text to Mr. Axler, "We have your package. We will meet you at the hotel as planned, Sir."

Mr. Axler smiles to himself. Checking his watch, he decides there is enough time to freshen up and order dinner. He sends a text to Captain Jim: "Send Miguel to pick me up in 2 hours and have the plane ready."

He orders room service then steps into the bathroom, very pleased that he will soon have the first skull. He has dreamed of this day for a very long time, ever since his grandfather shared the mystical ancient stories about the skulls and their power.

Raven and Grandma continue to chatter on in Spanish as Echo and Syd inhale the most amazing feast they ever tasted. There are home-made tortilla chips warm from the fryer, and they can not even put into words how amazing the fresh guacamole tastes.

Echo can't stop eating long enough to join in the conversation. "These chips and guacamole explode into a party of flavors with every bite," she finally manages to say.

Grandpa continues to bring trays of food out and place them on the table. Some dishes look familiar, others Echo doesn't recognize, but she tries some of each. She keeps getting side glances from Raven and Grandma; they have never seen someone so hungry. Echo shrugs and continues eating, enjoying the feast and the conversation.

Raven tells Grandma and Grandpa that they are on a girls' trip heading to Belize to visit some old friends. She apologizes for just showing up unannounced, but she didn't know when they would be passing through. Apparently, Raven stayed here when she was back-packing through Mexico with their granddaughter and developed a very close bond with them.

Echo finally stops eating and glances over at Syd who has been very quiet since they arrived. She still looks completely whacked out, Echo reaches under the table, resting her hand on Syd's knee, sending her some reiki healing energy. Syd covers Echo's hand with hers, smiling as some color returns to her face. Echo finally feels like herself again. She can share some energy. *Aaaah, there she is! I see the sparkle return to her eyes,* Echo thinks to herself as Syd winks at her. All is well . . . for now.

Echo excuses herself. Her belly beyond full, she moves outside to their front porch, breathing in the ocean air. There is a gentle, cool breeze, a clear night sky full of stars twinkling above. Echo falls into a brief meditation, giving gratitude for their safety, as well as the two magnificent people who not only welcomed them in but shared a feast prepared with so much love.

Echo is always amazed to meet such beautiful people who not only love each other deeply but openly share with all they meet. As she breathes in and out, allowing all the gratitude and love to flow freely through, her thoughts turn to Misty. Where is she? Why hasn't she shown up? Echo feels responsible somehow, wondering if Misty went searching for her when she went missing? *No, that can't be right*, she realizes. *Misty was missing before I was lost in time.*

Echo continues gazing out at the stars, thinking of Misty, when she feels Syd behind her. Syd wraps her arms around Echo. They are so close, feeling as if they grew up together instead of worlds apart.

"Hey Syd, you feeling better?" Echo asks as she leans into the hug, feeling so much love for her sister.

"Yes, thank you. Looks like we will stay the night here, we can get an early start in the morning. Raven said it is about an eight-hour drive to Belize," Syd tells her.

"Good idea," Echo says "however, I'm still concerned."

"I know," Syd cuts her off. "I already took care of it, but let's do one more together just to be sure."

Syd and Echo walk hand-in-hand off the porch and out into the yard and begin whispering a protective incantation.

As they go back inside to say goodnight, Grandpa—or "Papi" as Raven so lovingly calls him—is headed out the back door carrying two huge pitchers. Echo looks at Syd and says "I have a feeling it is some type of wonderful concoction probably involving tequila. I'm going to sleep like a baby tonight."

Raven tells Syd and Echo, "I have decided we should sleep outside in the backyard. Papi built a deck behind their home that could be in a magazine, come and see."

"Wow!" Echo and Syd say at the same time as they step outside.

The floorboards create a diamond design, The wood is as smooth as glass. The steps leading up to the deck are subtly lit from underneath; it is not bright at all, just enough glow to see the steps, giving the appearance the deck is floating. To the right is a stone area, with stone benches and a fire pit he built from stones he found on their land.

Papi is making a fire for them and Abuela is laying out a pallet of blankets and pillows.

Echo eyes begin to overflow with happy tears for the magical deck and garden Papi built. The warmth, kindness, and love from these two beautiful souls leaves them speechless.

"Buenas noches, Mijas," the couple says in unison as they hug each of the sisters and walk hand-in-hand into their lovely home.

Alone now, sitting by the fire, they reach out and hold hands, breathing in deeply and then out as if they are one. Their voices barely a whisper they begin to chant:

"We now cover thee with protection from above.

We cover thee with light with love.

We cover thee with protection from below.

We cover thee with this gift we bestow.

Flowing deep this protection surrounds.

Filled with love that abounds.

Keep thee safe from any harm.

Covered by our infinite charms."

They continue sitting by the fire, breathing in and out, just enjoying the beauty and each other. It is the first time they have had a chance to relax. For Raven and Syd, it has been a long day. For Echo it feels like weeks. None of them want this moment to end.

As the fire begins to die down, Echo is the first to break the silence. "I have to let you know what happened today. I didn't realize there were more than the empty faces after the skulls. Did either of you?" Echo says reluctantly. She realizes how silly she is in thinking that now that she has voiced it out loud.

Syd so quietly says, "Yes, there are many, and not just from our universe and time."

"Did y'all know that I touched the other skull and disappeared this morning?" Echo looks up into their faces lit by the fire.

Raven and Syd say at the same time, "Yes, sort of. How long were you gone?"

"I have no idea, when I touched the skull I was thrown back in time, I think. It was the ruins, but they weren't ruined, there was a village. Well, I am not sure what to call it, because there was no life at all, no sound there. It was a non-place, confusing." Echo continues telling them the entire story.

"Wow!" Raven said. "I think I know the girl. I believe it could be the Pepper I met long ago. I am not sure who the guy is. Any idea if they followed you here?"

"If they did, it wasn't with me or they would have landed there in the room. I have been practicing becoming time instead of bending it, although I have never been completely successful until today. I still have no idea how long I was gone. I do know it had to be a few days, at least that is what my body is telling me." Echo laughs, thinking of her stomach noises earlier. "We better get some sleep. I am so grateful we have each other." She says through a yawn.

As they recline under the stars, drifting off to sleep, they each begin to whisper their intentions. Echo plans to stay inside her body tonight to get a full night's sleep and recharge her mind, body, and soul. She wanted to share her thoughts about Misty with her sisters. As she snuggles into the wonderful, cozy beds Grandma made, with a full tummy, exhaustion takes over, and she drifts off to sleep, smiling with her heart full of joy.

SYD SETS HER INTENTIONS TO SLEEP TONIGHT and not get lost in her thoughts. She, too, is wondering where Misty is as she needs her help to decipher this language that she hears when she is near the skull. She feels so odd around them and then she can not exactly remember how she was able to remove the skull. Feeling exhausted, Syd drifts off to sleep.

RAVEN IS THE LAST OF THE SISTERS TO FALL asleep, she gazes up at the stars, wondering why Misty hasn't shown up, as she remembers their last conversation together. Misty told her she would meet them at the ruins.

CHAPTER 9

The sun begins to peak over the horizon at dawn, full of every color imaginable, covering the sky with the first glimmers of daylight.

Echo stirs awake, stretching her body, looking up into this display of indescribable colors. She thinks how blessed they are to live on this planet and yet so many people never stop to gaze upon it.

Echo lays there quietly in meditation, watching the sun's art display across the sky as Earth awakens to another day. Echo feels so grateful for this experience and begins setting her intentions for the day. "I intend for us to have a safe and stress-free journey today," Echo whispers quietly.

She sits up laughing as she hears the very same intention coming out in stereo from Raven and Syd who are lying on each side of her. "OH, GLORY BE!" Echo exclaims, laughing. "How wonderful to have you here, my lovely sisters, I love you so."

They all begin folding and stacking the many blankets and pillows. They know they must get moving as they have a long journey ahead of them. They hear Abuela singing in the kitchen—a wonderful Spanish melody as they carry in the last of the bedding. Such love flows from her, they are sad to leave. The tears already flowing from all of them as they say thank yous and goodbyes. Abuela has packed a feast for them to take, and they are forever grateful for the love and kindness this couple has shown them.

"No, no adios," Papi says, shaking his finger at them, "hasta luego, mi amor."

"We intend a safe and uneventful journey," Echo states as she starts the SUV.

Raven smiles at her and once again points the way as they head back out onto the highway.

"We are heading to Belize. Tapir Mountain Nature Preserve is our next location," Raven tells them as she folds up the map.

"I must tell you all that Misty has disappeared off my radar," Echo blurts out.

"I feel it, too," Syd and Raven say almost in unison.

"On my flight over, I was thinking back trying to remember the last few conversations I had with Misty to see if there is a clue as to where she may have gone. I even had some very old memories pop up from before I knew she was our sister, you know, previous lifetimes when she would show up and save me," Echo says, laughing out loud as if this was an everyday occurrence. "I know there has to be some way to figure out what happened. I can feel it, but I just can't seem to remember," she rambles on.

"Interesting, Echo, I feel the same way. I, too, was thinking back over our history on my flight here. I was wondering if Misty would go with us on our adventures or just pop in and out as she often does," Raven said.

"A few months ago, I had to visit Middle Earth. There was a message I needed to deliver. I saw Misty there, but it was odd. She was scattered, fading in and out sort of." Raven shakes her head and continues with her story. "I asked her if she was okay. Misty said she was looking for her mother, the Borteck had taken her but she was too late. Then, she faded away again."

"The Borteck . . . I remember Misty telling me about them as well! Didn't they disappear during the Middle Earth wars?" Syd chimes in.

"Yes, they did go into hiding, but considering what happened to Echo yesterday, I have my suspicions they have returned to find the skulls," Raven said. "I have not had a chance to tell you, the reason I went to Middle Earth was that the unicorns discovered an open portal that leads to several dimensions. Queen Andrea believes it is the work of the Borteck, and she requested my help to monitor the opening into our world. I have some friends taking care of that for me while I am away."

"My last visit with Misty we discussed the Borteck. She said after El Meco we had to go on to Belize and find the Actun Cave. Misty told me I will gather more information once there," Syd chimes in quietly.

"Syd, tell us what you know about the skulls," Echo says.

"Misty told me that alien races came to Earth long ago to help the human race advance. They first came in flying ships, and, of course, they were thought of as Gods. There were many races, but the crystal skulls were the most advanced. They all came and worked with Earth's Rulers throughout history—sharing knowledge, tools, building pyramids, and other portals which allowed them to go between Earth and their planet quickly.

"Misty wasn't sure exactly what changed, but she knew the crystal skull people were in grave danger. They came here trying to save their advanced knowledge. These thirteen leaders and their people came to Earth and, to protect themselves, shifted into a more human form so they could live here.

"These aliens were crystal inside with some sort of shimmery gray skin on the outside. They had long skulls and thin bodies. When they took human forms, they looked the same as humans on Earth, except they were still crystal on the inside. They lived here on Earth for several decades. Over time, they had children who were part human, part crystal. She thinks when the Middle Earth wars began and many of our magical races had to go into hiding, the hunt for the crystal skulls race began. They divided into small tribes, separating the thirteen forefathers. Misty believes the discovery of Actun was, in fact, one of the crystal skulls tribes," as Syd continues on with her story, the others can hear the pain in her voice.

"Actun Tunichil Muknal, which translates to the Cave of the Crystal Sepulchre, is where they found several skeletons, infants up to adults, the oldest of all was forty-five years old. Many of the children's skulls were elongated. Most of them were killed from a blow to the skull, or their entire skulls were crushed. The one I need to see is that of an eighteen-year-old girl. Her entire skeleton is crystal and calcified to the floor of the cave. Her skull was not crushed, but it appears her back was broken. She is now known as the Crystal Maiden.

"Legend tells us that the Mayans believed them all to be witches. Others believe they were Mayan Death Gods, but the locals refer to them as the Lords of Xibalba. Some even believe that this cave is an entrance to Hell. The ruins in this cave have been left untouched since they were discovered in the late 1980s. The only way into the cave is to hire a guide. It is an hour's drive and then at least an hour hike or more, as it requires you to swim in and then wade up a river through the jungle for a kilometer," Syd tells us.

They drive along in silence for quite a while, each lost to their own thought about the next journey. It will not be an easy one, which explains the supplies Misty asked Echo to buy.

They spot a small town along the way.

"I am going to stop up here. I need coffee and to stretch my legs," Echo says as she checks the gas gauge. "Oh, and gas would be helpful!"

"Oh good, I need to use the loo," Syd says, blushing.

They all laugh together, which immediately helps lift the mood. "I think we all need a pit stop," Raven says stretching. "Oh, and I can't wait to see what Abuela packed for us, I am a bit hungry."

Raven offers to drive as she has noticed how exhausted Echo looks. Echo is grateful, realizing she must have been gone longer than she thought and possibly what effects that laser thingy had on her body because she feels completely drained of all energy.

They fill up the SUV with gas and find a shady spot to enjoy the basket of food Abuela and Papi packed.

"I'm sorry, Y'all, but I need a nap," Echo says, yawning as she stretches out in the back seat, wishing she would have packed a travel pillow. She immediately falls asleep listening to Raven telling Syd about her past travels to Belize.

CHAPTER 10

"Oh, my goodness!" Echo says sitting up and stretching. "How long was I asleep for?"

"Just a little less than two hours," Syd says, turning around to look at Echo with a smile. "Did you get any sleep, Syd? The time change must be catching up to you?" Echo asks.

"No, I didn't, but I think I will definitely be in bed early tonight. We found a country house to rent that looks perfect. There are weather warnings on the radio; it looks like a tropical storm is heading this way, and we decided we better get off the roads," Syd tells her.

"Sounds good to me," Echo says.

Raven adds, "Yes, when they said the storm

is heading directly for Belize, Syd decided we had better stop as soon as we can. She found a great place for us to stay and has already called them to tell them we're coming. The woman, uhm, Julie? She told her there is a family that lives out on the property, so we can arrive at any time."

"Let's stop again, fill up with gas, and get some snacks and water," Syd suggests.

"Yes, it sounds like we are all going to need some rest," Echo tells them as she searches for information on her iPad about their next journey. "This trip to the cave is going to be quite an adventure, maybe the caretakers can help us locate a good guide."

"Yeah, according to our new friend, Julie, the family that takes care of her country home grew up in Belize. She said his name is Neysha, and he will make sure we have everything we need for a comfortable stay," Syd tells them.

All three sisters are beginning to feel effects of the first mission and are looking forward to relaxing this evening. Riding along in a peaceful silence, enjoying the beautiful scenery of Belize, they are in awe of this amazing place. They feel beyond blessed to be a part of this journey.

After a few stops to look at the paper map, as the internet and cell service is becoming unreliable, they finally find the home they rented, which couldn't be more perfect for them.

Echo breaks the silence. "I am always so delighted to see what the universe brings us when we allow it."

As Raven pulls into the driveway, the first thing they see is a large wooden welcome sign painted with tropical flowers of bright orange, yellow, and pink. The drive up the dirt road, which is lined with white stones on both sides and palm trees that have twinkle lights wrapped around the trunk, making it look like a magical fairy tale.

The home is painted bright orange with white trim, which stands out against all the lush green tropical plants. It has a large front porch. There, on the porch, is a very tall, dark, handsome man waving to them as he steps off the porch to greet the women.

"Hello. Welcome. I am Neysha," he says. His voice is deep, smooth and, with the native island accent, it sounds like a jazz song.

"Hello! I'm Raven, this is Syd and Echo,"

she says as they each reach out their hands to shake his. Instead, he pulls them into a group hug full of such warmth and gentleness—which is surprising as he is solid muscle. Gentle giant comes to Echo's mind; this man is a very old soul, she can feel his love for all living things.

"Come, I will show you da home. I have started a fire for you. The storms bring cold winds. My wife, Tillie, will bring you supper. Come come."

They follow him inside. Just as he said, there is a fire in the fireplace which casts a soft glow into the room rich with wood floors and soft yellow painted walls. It is decorated perfectly with a mix of tropical flare and some gorgeous artwork.

"Down the hall are three bedrooms. Please, go look around. I will bring da luggage," Neysha tells them, his voice filling the house with his rich jazzy sounds.

As they each choose their rooms, Raven tells Neysha where to place the suitcases. He is followed into the house by his wife.

Tillie is a petite woman. She is stunning— her skin a glowing golden brown with the slightest hint of pink as if she has just come in from the beach. She smiles shyly. "I am Tillie," she says very slowly, struggling with each word, her accent is different from Neysha's.

"Hello, Tillie," the sisters say in unison which is followed by giggles. Neysha and Tillie begin to laugh as well as they walk out.

"I am going to go get my comfies on," Syd says, laughing all the way down the hallway.

Raven and Echo have just settled down by the fireplace when there is a knock at the door. Echo jumps up to open the door, and she sees Neysha and Tillie. Tillie is carrying a platter full of a delicious display of fruits and veggies.

"Come in," Echo says as she opens the door wide.

Tillie is followed in by Neysha with a large platter full of several different types of dishes. The smell is like a party of flavors filling the room. Echo's stomach rumbles loudly. Neysha looks down at her and smiles. "Enjoy. We will see you in da mornin'."

"Wow, thank you so much!" Raven and Echo say excitedly.

"Welcome, I have closed da shutters already, a storm is coming some time in da night. Take this," he says as he hands Raven a walkie talkie. "Just press the button and talk, okay?"

"Yes, thank you," Raven says looking at the walkie talkie. "I remember having these when I was a kid. How fun."

They decide to sit around the fire to enjoy the feast. Echo searches the kitchen for dishes and finds a bottle of wine. Raven spreads a blanket and pulls over the small coffee table. Syd comes out to join them, grabs the throw pillows off the couch, and places them around the table to sit on. These three beautiful women only just met in person a few days earlier and yet are so deeply connected. It's as if they were born and raised together—triplets.

"Misty would absolutely be here if she could. I know we will find her," Echo says quietly.

"But for now, let's enjoy this precious moment." Echo raises her wine glass for a toast.

They enjoy their amazing dinner, fine wine, and conversation inside their cozy cottage while the beginnings of the storm start to blow in. The rain and winds hit the metal shutters, which, surprisingly, makes a low drumming sound. They hear occasional rumblings of thunder—Mother Earth's symphony. How blessed they are to be together, safe, and sheltered from the storm.

They are startled by Neysha's voice booming over the walking talkie. "Ladies, just letting you know da storm is a big one, but you are safe. Just plan on staying inside, this storm may last a few days, okay?"

Raven is already up and moving toward the walkie talkie; she has reflexes like a cat. "Yes, thank you, Neysha," Raven tells him. "Looks like our plans have changed, dear ones," she turns toward the others, smiling, her eyes sparkling like stars in the dark sky.

CHAPTER 11

"You're wearing a path in the floor with your pacing, Brother," Kyle says concerned.

Jake looks over at his brother as he continues pacing. "It has been five days and not one word from her," he says. "It's so not like her at all, if nothing else, she always checks in on the ranch."

"Well, the airlines said her flight landed without problems, and she was on it, right? You checked the car rental, and she picked up a vehicle, right? So, my guess is she is having fun with her sisters and lost track of time. Come on, Jake, you know how that goes; we have done it a time or two," Kyle said smiling. "Let's get the animals fed; it will calm you down. Then, if you still haven't heard from her, we will figure out a plan."

"Thank you for coming out to help me, Kyle. I appreciate it. Okay, if I don't hear from Echo by tomorrow, I am going to go look for her. I just feel like something is not right," Jake says, rubbing his hands through his thick curls—an old habit he adopts when he tries to solve a problem.

Kyle wraps an arm around Jake's shoulders, pulling him into a hug. "It's been too long since we have had an adventure together." Jake doesn't know yet that Kyle has some girl troubles of his own. Kyle isn't about to share right now, as he has never seen his brother so tied up in knots over a woman, but he wonders if there is more than a working relationship going on between the two.

Once their ranch chores are complete, he will make a good dinner, and they can catch up. Kyle loves to cook, and Echo's kitchen is a chef's dream. It surprises him as Echo hates to cook yet has all the very best cooking gadgets. "Let's go, Jake. We're burning daylight," Kyle says as he lets out a deep laugh.

Jake joins in the laughter as they walk down the path to the barn before growing serious once again. "I just can't shake the feeling she's in danger."

TO BE CONTINUED. . .

GET READY FOR BOOK TWO!

Jake has plans to leave the ranch and search for Echo. . .

. . .until he receives papers informing him that he is the only living guardian for his orphaned half sister, True.

Jake never knew much about his father because he took off when Jake and Kyle were kids. He has to meet them at the courthouse, but is delayed at the ranch gates by several men looking for Kyle.

Meanwhile. . .

As Echo searches for the second skull, she discovers she is in real danger.

The side effects of whatever Pepper shot her

with are showing up as she and Syd explore the underground world of the crystal caves.

Mayan legend says these caves are a portal between the human world and the invisible world of the gods.

Raven has gone to Middle Earth to find help in the search for Misty and has discovered chaos still consumes Middle Earth.

What kind of dangers await them?

You'll love the second installment of the adventures of these cosmic twinkle sisters because of the twists, turns, and fast-paced action!

ACKNOWLEDGMENTS

RECOGNITION. . .
    WITH GRATITUDE. . .

To my precious angels, Kyle and Jacquelyn, who listened to my crazy stories and "never-grow-up attitude" while I raised them. I often wondered who raised whom?

You two gifts are a part of my heart, my soul, and I could not have managed this life without you. My greatest blessing and joy is to be your momma. You amaze me each and every day—I love you forever and always.

My parents for their unconditional love and

guidance. They always believed in me and encouraged me to chase my dreams and to DREAM BIG.

My circle of friends, my sisters, and cosmic sisters—I love you so much. Thank you for encouraging me to be the best me I can be, and for allowing me to share some of our stories woven into the magic of this book.

Thank you to my editor, Qat Wanders—without your patience, guidance, and talent, my stories would never be shared with the world.

Thank you, Mandi J. Miller, for the amazing photographs.

ABOUT THE AUTHOR

A former physical therapist, K.J. currently devotes most of her time to caring for her mother. She is an online spiritual teacher, life coach, and story-teller. She raised two fabulous children and, in her spare time, wrote short stories. K.J. loves to travel and discover fabulous places to immerse herself in the local culture and cuisine.

You can read her blog at
www.kjking.org
or email her at
kjkinginvest@outlook.com